When the Clock Strikes Dead

a Jud Carson mystery

by John M. Spafford

When the Clock Strikes Dead

a Jud Carson mystery

Preface and Disclaimer:
Notebook 24, Entry 14

All of the characters in this tale are real. The people that they're based on are all fictitious. Figure it out for yourself.

Notebook 24, Entry 15

Sure, the gap between what is and what a client comes to me for is generally only slightly wider than the Grand Canyon. And it's generally only a little less than impossible to being something that they are going to step across to getting.

I've been measuring that gap for clients who thought that they could walk on air for long enough to be able to spot just how many have a chance of putting my talents to work and getting everything that they want for a pile of nothing in return. I can count their number comfortably on no fingers of either hand.

That doesn't stop the fairly steady stream of men and women – mostly women – who want me to solve their problems in a matter of minutes armed with nothing but a few bucks and a lot of lies. And knowing it doesn't stop me from taking the cases, spending the cash and pretending that I believe the lies that they tell me – while they pretend I don't know that nearly everything that comes out of their mouths is lies.

Most of what I deal with is agony and greed and treachery and pettiness – and the first casualty of those – just as in war – is truth.

I'm going to tell enough lies in this version of the truth to make it tough, if not impossible, to hang a rap on me for telling tales out of school.

Jud Carson, P.I.
San Francisco

Notebook 24 Entry 16

"It's just a helluva damned no-good thing," Stu Allgood said to no one in particular.

"Your bangtail come in last again?" I asked.

I had crossed the lobby of my hotel of residence and come up on the house detective's blind side. The doctor had done a good job. Except for a lack of luster the glass eye matched up pretty well and most people didn't twig unless he forgot to lift the shade on that side.

"I wish it was just that," Stu said. "I wish to hell-and-a-half that I never got another winner rather than this."

I studied him and then shook my head. "So are you going to let me in on the tragedy?" I asked at last. "Or do I have to wait to read about it in the rags?"

"You mean to tell me that an in-the-know guy like you isn't already on the inside of this?" He turned on me and shook his head. "I would have thought that you would know before me! A helluva-damned thing like this!"

"Stu, tell me what is going on."

"Danny Granger," he said simply. "He's dead. Took three in the chest in his very own damned living room."

My gut turned over. Granger and I had known each other for a lot of years. A few years older than me, he had tossed me occasional work when I was still a green op. He'd done that for a lot of guys, just to keep us in the business and off of the soup or factory line.

"Now aint that a helluva damned no-good thing?" Stu asked.

My lights dimmed for an instant. Then I squared my shoulders and turned away. "Yeah," I said. "It's a helluva damned no-good thing." I started across the lobby toward the elevator on the far wall.

"She's up there waiting for you," Stu said from behind me.

I turned. "Who is?"

"Dixie," he said. "I told her she could wait for you up there."

A couple of minutes later I was walking from the elevator toward Dixie LaBlanc, already in widow's black, sitting on the small couch in the sitting room of the fifth floor.

"I'm sorry – " I started but Dixie waived my sympathy off.

"Danny always said to make sure that you got – this – stuff. I found some more and just put it in – whatever was on his desk – I didn't want the dicks going through his things." There was a sniffle that told me tears were close to the surface.

"Was Danny onto something?" I asked. I found that I was avoiding looking at the box. It was like looking into his grave and I wasn't ready to do that just yet.

Dixie shrugged. "Dan was always onto

something. You know that."

I nodded. "What about the cops?" I pursued. "Do they have anything?"

"Not much. I was doing a show, so it was just Dan and the killer at our place. A neighbor called the cops when he heard the shots."

"See anything?"

She shook her head. "Probably hiding in a closet."

"At least he called," I offered.

"Yeah, at least. Could of maybe come and – tried – "

"Hey, Dix," I said, "from what I hear, it was delivered before he knew it was in the mail."

I had more questions but I just couldn't bring myself to ask them.

"Dixie, why don't you come down to my place and we can talk?" I offered. "I've got some 12-year-old Scotch that needs to express itself." I wasn't all that comfortable being around a dead colleague's squeeze so soon after he had had his ticket punched, but I couldn't just say 'Thanks for coming by' and leave it at that, either. I owed Dixie more than that. And I sure as hell owed Danny Granger more than that.

But I didn't have to worry. With a shrug Dixie had turned and started for the elevator. "Too bad you didn't make that offer when Danny was still alive," she said. "We could have had some laughs."

She walked away and made it count but only in

the 'could-have-been' way that means it sure as hell doesn't have a chance of being anymore. I had to admit that I could admire the packaging even though I wouldn't want to unwrap it. Every vice has a limit and I was pretty sure that I had learned most of mine a long time ago.

I picked up the box and made my way to my rooms. I put it on the kitchen counter and went into the living room. I needed a stiff drink before I started going through Danny's life. I passed up the 12-year-old that was reserved for special guests. The cheap, raw stuff would suit the moment better.

Without the box obscuring my view I could see the small ivory-colored envelope that had been slipped under my door sometime earlier. I picked it up and poured my drink, slammed it down and poured another before breaking the seal. Inside was a note that named a time and place. I figured it must be from someone who shared my convictions because the sender had included a dollar sign at the bottom.

Notebook 24, Entry 17

Two of Lt. Martinelli's homicide squad, Crayton and Russell, fell in beside me the instant that I stepped onto the sidewalk and guided me to the waiting squad car parked in the alley. Martinelli was in the front passenger seat and I was hustled into the back with a linesman on either side. The tight squeeze made it hard to breathe. The cheap cologne made it worse.

"Which one of you is running the whorehouse?" I asked.

Martinelli rolled his eyes and sighed. "Cut the comedy, Carson," he said. "We've got to have a chat about your pal Danny Granger."

"Nice guy," I said. "Paid his taxes. Stayed in the middle of his lane."

"Don't give me that," the lieutenant snapped. "Granger was as easy on the edges as the rest of you peepers."

"He didn't deserve to get capped off in his own house in front of the picture of his sainted mother," I said.

Martinelli flexed his jaw.

"He saved your ass a time or two," I went on.

The cop held up a hand to cut me off. He gestured and the driver and two side men got out of the car. They moved to the head of the alley and began to talk amongst themselves.

"Yeah," Martinelli said at last, "Granger did me

some solids. He did that for a bunch of us."

"And?"

"And I don't need a bunch of P.I.s running around looking to settle scores."

I settled back. So that was it. He was putting us on notice that we were to defer to the S.F.P.D. on the case of Daniel Lawrence Granger.

"So you expect us to just trade bubblegum cards and wait while the slow wheel of justice grinds?"

Martinelli's eyes narrowed and his nostrils flared. It might have made him look funny except for the fact that I knew just how dangerous he could be. This was no dumb flat-foot made rank. He was as tough as they came and knew just how close to the edge of the cliff he could dance.

"Any leads?" I asked.

Martinelli shook his head. "I was going to ask you the same thing."

"Nothing. Just found out. What do you know?"

"Small caliber. Close range. Pretty much instantaneous. He never had a chance."

"You know what that means, don't you?" I asked.

"Yeah," Martinelli said. "It means that Granger knew the shooter."

We were silent for a moment. Then, "I need to know that you and your friends will steer clear of this."

"And feed you what we get."

"Look, Carson, I don't need your help! And if I

did…" He stopped, shook his head and seemed to gather his thoughts again. "Yeah, whatever you get," he said.

I nodded and Martinelli signaled for his men to return. Crayton opened the back door to let me out. "Sorry about Granger," he said softly.

I nodded again. "You still smell like a whorehouse," I said.

The crimson silk Chinese dress was split on the side from the floor to her collar. Three tasseled silk cords tied in bows held it together: one on the creamy skin of her right hip, one half-way up her ribcage, and one between her shoulder and neck.

A mandarin collar with three pearl buttons stood at attention under a delicate chin. The diamond shape of her face seemed to float above the dress, and the green of her eyes matched that of the dragon, accented with gold threads, that wrapped around her waist and curled upward, its open mouth perched on the seat of honor commanding the view from her right breast.

Her dark auburn hair cascaded down around her shoulders and for a moment I wondered, like most of the other men in the room, what it would be like to be hidden, even lost, in that veil. She seemed so unaware of the effect that she had on a room that there was no doubt that she knew exactly what effect she was having.

"Mr. Carson?" she asked. Her voice was silk

rustling on silk. The dress and hairstyle were out of the Far East, but her accent was Back Bay, with touches of a dozen ports of call since. She had been around all right, but always on her own terms.

I stood and nodded once, then pulled out the chair next to me.

"Have I kept you waiting long?"

I wondered how she would manage the chair in the suggestion of a dress that she was wearing. It didn't take long to get an answer: Very well.

"No, just long enough," I said. I gestured for the waiter and when he leaned over I whispered 'Two bourbon and branch' in keeping with the former speakeasy's tradition.

"I suppose that you want me to get right to the point," she went on.

"Not especially," I said. "I haven't had my drink yet and I'm enjoying the atmosphere. But if you have somewhere to go...someone to meet..."

"No," she said softly as she glanced around, "it's nothing like that. But, do you think that we are safe here?"

I took a look around.

"Safe is a relative term. Miss – ?" I raised my eyebrows to emphasize the point that I hadn't been told what to call her yet.

"Merriman," she offered. "Elaine Merriman."

I smiled and nodded.

" – Merriman." I picked up where I had put the

hole in our conversation. "I'd say that we were safe from most things. Excluding earthquakes and tourists. This is San Francisco, after all."

She glanced around again, this time with more of an apparent concern.

"Look, Miss – " I paused to get a grip on the name that she had given me – "Merriman"

Her eyes darted back at me like twin vipers.

"You say that like you don't believe me," she said.

"Believe you?"

"That my name is Elaine Merriman."

I sighed, smiled and shook my head. This was becoming comical. Thankfully, the waiter arrived just in time to break the rhythm of the conversation. After he had placed the drinks, collected, and left, I stirred the brown liquid for a few seconds.

"Quite frankly, I don't care if you call yourself 'Mary Astor'," I said. "I was asked to meet you here to discuss a possible job. That's the extent of my concern." I took a sip of my drink and sat back.

She seemed to be considering things. Then, "I am sorry, Mr. Carson, I didn't mean to be rude. It's just that I'm frightened. And alone."

This was a dame that would only be alone when she wanted it that way, I thought. She was as curvy as Lombard Street. And as intriguing. The man who could master the two of them would have a lot to brag about. I had already driven Lombard.

"That's okay," I soothed. "Just relax and tell me all about it."

"There is a letter," she began.

I nodded.

"A man named Brighton, Jeffrey Brighton, he has it. He stole it from me and I must have it back." She lowered her eyes then used the straw to sip from her drink.

"And you would like me to make sure that that happens?"

She looked up at me with those green eyes under the veil of her lashes. The straw was still in place in the cupid's bow of her mouth. When she set the glass down there was a suggestion of her crimson lipstick on the straw.

"I spoke to some people who said that you are the type of man I need."

"And you trust those people to know the type of man that you need." I didn't ask – I just laid it out like a low off-suit to see what shook out of the bushes.

"Yes," she said simply. She met my eyes but she wasn't giving anything away.

"Very well," I said, "now let's suppose that I am the kind of man that you need. And let's suppose that I locate Jeffrey Brighton and ask for your letter back." I took a sip of my bourbon and branch, considered for a moment, then went on. "And let's suppose that he says that he doesn't want to do that." I looked her in the eyes. "What then?"

She didn't hesitate for more than a breath. "I was told, by some people," she said, "that you were a man who knew what to do. And that you were able to handle anything that came your way." She seemed to sit up a bit more straight and the dragon's mouth seemed to open a bit more as she pulled her shoulders back and thrust his perch further out.

I tightened my upper lip across my teeth and nodded slowly. So that was it, was it? Someone had put her on to me because the word was that I knew how to shave the edges from the letter of the law and still get the desired results. Or maybe she had been told that I wasn't above dealing from the bottom of the deck if that's what it was going to take to make rent.

I shook off the implied insult and turned my attention back to the moment. So this letter was that important to her. Well, maybe it was and maybe it wasn't. The question was how important it was going to be to me. I looked at the dragon again and wondered why it was that I seldom got the kinds of things coming my way that I would enjoy.

From somewhere she had produced five Franklins and placed them on the table between us. Normally I don't like crowds but the seven of us seemed to make for a cozy time.

"Is this enough to get things started?" she asked.

I looked at the bills and then up at her again. She was a cool one, all right. She had trouble written all over her in a half-dozen languages. I read danger on her like a blind man knows to stand still when his cane stops tapping out the safe step.

She was the kind of woman that could melt you with her kisses and still have ice in her spine. And the man who held her in his arms, even knowing that she was that kind of a woman, would feel lucky.

I told myself that I should get up, walk away and never look back. There was enough cash in the roll stashed behind my kitchen stove for me to take a week off and head out of town in case she tried to change my mind. I could suggest a couple of other private eyes who could use the work and weren't discriminating about the source of it. I even knew a couple who deserved to spend time in her company and suffer whatever was going to fall on their heads from the association.

But the dragon on her breast grinned at me as if it already knew my next words.

"What can you tell me about Jeffrey Brighton?" I asked.

Notebook 24, Entry 18

I had spotted the tail as I slipped Elaine Merriman's phone number – I recognized it as one of the city's finer hotels – into my pocket and before I could even consider how I was going to track Jeffrey Brighton down in a city the size of San Francisco.

He was too big to be doing that kind of work and the tweed jacket that he wore was expensive and well-tailored but you wouldn't know it by the way that he had stretched it over his broad back and chest. It made him almost like a parody. The obvious bulge of a rod under his left arm decreased my sense of levity. He was doing his best to look inconspicuous at the news and tobacco stand across from the *Bourbon and Branch* but he might as well have been waiving a flag for all the good it did.

It didn't take a team from Stanford to figure out the play. He had followed her to the speak and seen her meet with me. Now he would tag one of us and I had a feeling that he already knew something about Elaine Merriman that I had not – where she was hanging her glad rags when it was time to call it a full day of intrigue. That meant that he would be more likely to try to cut sign on me instead. I walked to the corner and turned toward the bay. It would be easier for him to keep track of me if I were going down the hill. At least it would be until I decided just how I wanted to play him.

My hunch turned out and I could hear him

● ● ●

crossing the damp street behind me. A minute later I started making a series of zig-zags along the narrowing streets: first a turn to the west, then one to the north. They weren't obvious moves to shake a tail, in fact, my pace hadn't picked up at all. But I knew where I was going and what I was going to do when I got there. My traveling companion was, figuratively, in the dark.

Then the lights did go out for him when I turned into an alley, slipped down a half-flight of stairs and pushed through the unlocked delivery door of my favorite laundry. I leaned against the door and listened for him to enter the alley. When he did I could sense his frustration. There was nowhere to turn out of the alley for quite a ways and yet he couldn't see me up ahead. It took only a few seconds for him to realize and accept that he had managed to lose me. All right. Now what? Do what thugs always do: go back to the one with the brain and let them figure it out. His shoe leather scuffed and he turned about face.

I was much better at following a mark than he was. He didn't figure that out during the half an hour that we walked.

The boy was off duty and there was a neat sign that advised "Self-Service Hours" were in effect when I watched the goon step into the walnut-lined Otis elevator. The car stopped at the sixth floor. I nodded to Tom Geary, the house dick who was perched on the shoe-shine kid's chair, and then followed the tweed jacket up.

When the doors opened I turned to the right and made a quick case of the doors. Only two had lights shining under them. I checked the other end of the hall: one light on. I knocked. When the door opened I could see well into the room above the petite blonde's page-boy.

"Hmmm...room service is going to get a helluva tip!" she laughed. The left shoulder strap of her chemise slipped as she draped herself against the door and the top of a tear-drop shaped breast was revealed. The silk fabric was held up by what seemed to be a pencil eraser jutting out from behind the material.

As she shifted her weight back I glanced down. She had tiny, delicately shaped feet. The left one bent up at the joint of her toes and her heel rested against the edge of the door as she came to rest like a beautiful bird on a perch. Her toes were carefully lacquered a bubble-gum pink. It was a cinch that her paint would be a match for a couple of points of interest higher up.

She stretched slowly, arching her back against the door. It wasn't a big gesture but it was big enough to make sure that I got the message. Page-boy didn't believe in wearing panties.

Her lips parted and she mouthed "The lobby in thirty," to me then punctuated the invitation with a stab of her soft, pink tongue and a wink.

The man behind her, dressed in pajama bottoms and tattoos, didn't seem as amused. "Whatayawant?" he demanded.

"Sorry, folks, I guess I got the wrong room," I said quickly and backed away.

"Too bad," Page-boy said with a sigh and a pout as she was closing the door between us.

"Whataya mean by that?" the voice of Tattoos carried through as the door clicked.

I crossed to the other end of the hall, glanced along the corridor, then quickly put my ear to the first door. A radio hissed that the station selected had gone off the air. I moved to the next suspect apartment. Muffled voices.

I took a deep breath and knocked. Nothing happened. I knocked again. Nothing, unless the fact that the voices suddenly fell silent counted as something. I raised my hand and prepared to use my knuckles again just as the door knob began to turn.

"Who the hell – " Tweed let the question die on his thick lips.

I gave him a broad wink and a smile. "Going to invite me in or should I just wait downstairs?" I asked.

Tweed's face flushed. "Boss," he said, "this is the guy."

A man who had been seated in an armchair directly behind the thug at the door stood up. Until he had moved I hadn't seen him at all. He was slight, had thinning blonde hair and a pencil-thin moustache.

"Hello, I am, as has just been pointed out, 'The Guy'," I said. "Or Jud Carson. And you are Jeffrey Brighton. We should talk."

When Tweed looked over his shoulder at Brighton for instructions I eased forward, slipped past him down the short entranceway and entered the suite's sitting room. Jeffrey Brighton extended a small, fine-boned hand. "I don't believe we have met," he said in a polite tone that spoke of breeding and education. Somewhere in there was the suggestion that he had also been around a lot of bad things in his life. More importantly to me, was the distinct impression that he had done some of them himself and not found it difficult to look in the mirror afterward.

Brighton nodded once to the man at the door and I could hear the latch set behind me. I moved forward, shook Brighton's hand noncommittally and let the hireling move past me. He took a chair on the other side of the room.

"It is a bit late for callers," Brighton said as he turned to the bar set up on the lowboy. His gesture offered whiskey. Mine accepted and he poured two fingers from a decanter into a pair of glasses. He didn't offer ice. The tweed jacket wasn't drinking.

"You can play cagey all you want," I said, taking a sip. It was decent booze. Not top shelf but not rot, either. "But we both know the game. Your man here saw me with Elaine Merriman tonight." A slight narrowing of his eyes told me that Brighton had never heard the name before. Okay, so it wouldn't be the first time that a client had given me a false moniker. I went on. "I figure that he followed her from her place, picked up my trail, and, well, we all know how that worked out because here I stand drinking your Irish."

"You are here about the letter," Brighton said. He gestured toward the chair behind me and I parked my tumbler on the end table, opened my trench coat, thumbed the button on my jacket open and accepted his second invitation. He waited until I had picked up my drink before seating himself across from me.

"That's the nut of it," I agreed as I raised my glass in a salute. "The letter."

Notebook 24, Entry 19

"I'm going to have to trust you – just a little," Brighton said. "I don't want to, but I don't see any other alternative at the moment." He put his glass down and leaned toward me. "Now that Miss 'Merriman'," he said the name carefully, as though trying to make sure that he didn't slip and use another, more familiar one, "no longer has it I suspect that she is desperate to get it back."

He smiled. "As for you, I don't think that you have any idea whatever about the letter. For all you know it is a letter of credit – or a political plan."

I nodded. "It could be a party invitation for all I know," I conceded. There was no use in denying it. A question or two at the most would have given Brighton all the evidence he needed that he was right. Besides, as long as he was talking, I was getting smarter. I had no intention of turning the tables.

"I didn't think she would be willing to share that information," he mused. Then, "Well, it is not," he went on. "It is something far more important. And more valuable."

I looked at my glass and waited until he was ready to go on.

"You've heard of Thomas Jefferson," he began slowly. "He wrote the Declaration of Independence."

I nodded. I could have added that the Virginia planter had been pretty heavily influenced by the

Swiss jurist Jean Jacques Burlamaqui, but there was no reason to let him think that I was any more educated than the average door knob that he was used to keeping company with. "Two dollar bill," I said.

"Same guy," Brighton agreed with a slight, knowing smile. He figured he had measured my depth and had decided that he wouldn't have to wade too deep to drown me in his intellect.

I looked at his insurance in the corner. "I got your name. And Jefferson's. He got a handle or does he just respond to whistles?" The rib-cracker stiffened slightly.

"What's in a name?" Brighton asked, his right hand, palm down gesturing subtly to his companion.

"A. An. Am. Me. Men. Man. Mean." I rattled off the seven words and then turned my attention to the thug again. "Mane. Amen."

Brighton raised an eyebrow and the corner of his mouth curled and twitched to let me know that he was more annoyed than amused.

I shrugged. Out of the corner of my eye I could see the too-tight tweed stretch as the man inside of it relaxed in the armchair. The mahaska bulged obscenely even in the low light of the room.

Brighton picked up the thread of his monologue again. "Jefferson has a lot of fans and a lot of foes. Some of those in each camp have been looking for a particular piece of evidence for a long time."

"The letter," I said.

"The letter," he agreed.

He nodded and sighed. For a moment he seemed to be considering just how much to tell me. "Jefferson had a slave – a beautiful young woman named 'Sally Hemmings'," he said at last.

"And?"

"And Jefferson may have been a genius and a patriot but he was still a slave owner." He raised an eyebrow again, this time as an unstated question.

"And he was a man," I answered.

Brighton rocked back and forth slightly in his chair. "Yes," he said. "And he was a man." He reached into his inside jacket pocket and when his hand reappeared it held a secretary-style wallet. From it he withdrew a piece of yellowed paper. He looked at it with obvious admiration before handing it across to me.

The image that stared back at me was what poets spend lifetimes trying to describe. I knew that I had about as much chance of putting into words the take-your-breath-away-and-leave-you-happier-for-it-beauty of the young black woman as I would in trying to strike out the Big Bambino, or of going fifteen with Sullivan. I wouldn't even try. Instead I would hope to burn the image into my brain so that when I no longer had the slip of paper I could keep some piece of her in my memory.

Men, God help me, even men like Jefferson, could be forgiven for being struck by the open, casual, and honest beauty of this long-dead woman. They could not be forgiven for enslaving her for their own desires. I handed the paper back with a mixture of regret and satisfaction. Regret that I could no longer look into the painter's no-doubt poor representation. Satisfaction that slavery was no longer a going concern.

"So, can you imagine," Brighton began, "what would happen if a letter, authenticated to be in Jefferson's handwriting, were to turn up and contain evidence that he had…" it was as though he was doing his best to not discuss the rotting carcass in the parlor.

"Been intimate?" I suggested.

"Fathered children," he answered more directly.

"With her?" I nodded toward the paper he still held.

"With a slave," he said. "It isn't that a white slave owner bedding a slave was so unheard of," Brighton went on. "It's a known fact that Hemmings was Jefferson's wife's half-sister."

"It's that it is Jefferson." I nodded.

People in both camps would want a letter like that for their own reasons, I thought. The pro-Jeffersonians would want it to show that he didn't let race get in the way of love. And he might have heirs whose mother had been the property of one of the country's most famous founding fathers. His detractors would love to ballyhoo it to diminish his influence. This sin could be used to paint Jefferson as a hypocrite and worse. 'All men are created equal,' and all of that.

"So you can see why it is so important."

I nodded slowly.

"And you can see why it is so valuable?" This was a question. He wanted to get me involved with the discussion and I wasn't sure that I liked what I thought it meant.

I sat back, whistled softly then glanced at the over-stuffed tweed in the corner. "Just seeing if you were still awake," I said. "Yeah," I went on, turning back to Brighton. "It would be worth a bunch of two-dollar bills."

"But the best money is going to come from the right people," Brighton said quickly.

"And you know who the right people are," I offered.

"Yes, yes, I do. So you see?"

"See?"

"See why I am willing to pay you – and pay you handsomely, I might add – for your assistance in getting that letter for me. I don't know if your client is simply shopping the article around or prepared to make a deal. And I can assure you, whatever your companion of this evening is offering, I am prepared to offer more than she."

Things had been going pretty well up till now. I hadn't seen this curve coming and I nearly rolled it when I tried to slam on the brakes. I hoped that my up-raised glass had provided enough cover that he didn't see my surprise at this revelation: He was in the letter *buying* end of the business, not the letter *having*. If he figured that the dame was trying to buy it, too, and was willing to out-bid her, then the question became letter, letter, who's got the letter?

"I've never made it to the 'handsome' level," I lied. "Just how good does 'handsome' look?"

"Shall we say twenty thousand dollars when the letter is in my hand? And more when I have transacted it with a buyer."

"And how much more would that be?"

"One-sixth of as much as a quarter of a million. Maybe more." He fixed me with his eyes as he waited for a commitment.

"Very well, let's say that," I answered by way of acceptance.

"A capable, resourceful, and wise man. I could have used your talents on many an occasion," Brighton said.

"And don't forget thrifty, kind, reverent and clean," I added. "But I don't have it, at least, not right now," I said.

"But you can get it." Brighton was eager now and I could see that his cool, detached manner only went so far. He was a kid at the circus with a fist full of Jeffersons.

I shrugged and stretched an eyebrow toward the ceiling then let it fall.

"You've been after this letter for a long time," I said.

"A very long time."

"You shouldn't have a problem waiting a little longer," I said as I pushed up from the chair.

"Don't make me wait too long, Mr. Carson," Brighton said. He leaned forward and smiled thinly. "I'd hate to have to reconsider my offer." His eyes flicked to the corner of the room where his goon sat, then they returned to settle on me. "I wouldn't want to start thinking that you are going into business for yourself."

I picked up my hat from the table and started for the hall.

"Don't bother to get up," I said. "I can find my own way." At the door I turned and twisted the knob, pulled and stepped half-way through the frame. "As far as going into the antique letters business, don't worry – I have enough to do with the business I'm in," I said. "You'll be hearing from me by tomorrow afternoon. Have your money ready. Cash, if you please. And not in two-dollar bills."

Notebook 24, Entry 20

It was staring at me from the moment that I opened my door. A dead detective had wanted me to have it for some reason. Dixie had made sure that I got it. Now it was time to deal with Danny Granger's box. I poured a drink and pulled the box between the coffee table and couch. On top was a black and white photo of several of us who made our living minding other people's business. Danny Granger had thrown a party when he had moved into his new house with Dixie a few years back. It had been a lot more fun than any of us wanted to admit. We were all a lot younger. There was less blood on our hands. I took a drink and set the photo aside.

There were case files, Danny's telephone register, his sister's address on a Christmas card that was four years old. The flotsam and jetsam of a private detective's life. At the bottom of the box was a slip of paper. Stapled to it was a pawn ticket for a leather briefcase. It was dated the day before Danny Granger had caught his last case. I picked up the green and black ticket, considered it for a moment and glanced at the clock. Still too early to get across town and see what this final pawn was about. Still, it wouldn't hurt to start getting ready. A shower and a shave, not to mention a fresh suit of clothes, would go a long way toward making me feel human again. It might even take the grit out of my eyes. I stood, dropped the pawn ticket on the table and was turning toward the bedroom when I heard the soft rapping on my door.

I wouldn't have been too surprised to find any number of people at my door. I more than half expected to find one of the other private dicks who made their living in the city standing there and ready to lay out a plan to settle the score with whoever it had been that ended Danny Granger's career. I wasn't prepared for the one that it turned out to be.

A moment later Elaine Merriman pushed the hood of her blue velvet cape back and smiled faintly. "Can I come in?" she asked.

I pushed the corners of my mouth down for an instant and nodded.

She stepped into the room and paused while I eased the cape from her shoulders. "You'll have to forgive me," I said, pointing to the empty Chesterfield. "It's the maid's year off."

She turned her head and smiled wanly. "I admire a man who can look after his own needs," she said. "It makes me feel more confident that he can take care of mine."

"I do what I can," I offered.

She crossed the room, glanced at Granger's box and contents, then turned back to me. "I suppose," she began, "you must wonder why I am here at this hour."

I shook my head slightly. "I try not to wonder too much, Miss Merriman. I find that it takes the surprise out of life."

"Please, you simply must call me 'Elaine'," she said. She glanced around again and I wondered if she was looking for a place to perch. Then she tossed her head and gave me another strained smile. "Well, the fact is, after you left, I saw a man follow you. I wasn't sure, of course, that isn't my line of work, but I was pretty sure. So – "

"So you came here to warn me," I said.

She bit her lower lip and nodded. "You must think me very silly, Mr. Carson."

"Not at all, Elaine," I said, crossing to her. "And please, you simply must call me 'Jud'."

We stood facing each other for a moment. Then, "There is something else that I was wondering about," she said.

"What is that?"

"How it would feel to kiss you," she said. Then her chin tilted to just the right kiss-me angle and her breath was on my mouth as I descended to answer her curiosity.

For several minutes we busily satisfied our interests. At last I stepped back and let my arms release their hold on her willing body.

"And?" I asked.

"And I am glad that I caught you when I did," she said, one hand touching her hair and the other smoothing her dress. "It looks as though you were getting ready for bed and if I had arrived any later it would have been very embarrassing for me to leave here several hours from now."

"I don't know, I have a very understanding landlord," I said.

"Good night, Jud," she said, leaning forward for a final kiss.

I locked the door after her and headed for the shower. I was going to have to postpone my trip to the pawn shop or find another way to get that errand seen to.

Notebook 24, Entry 21

I looked at the note again. She had a firm, graceful script that could have been lifted from an engraver's folio; the blue ink staining the ivory note-paper with carefully controlled strokes and gentle flourishes spoke of business and intimacy at once. The faint aroma of jasmine laced the paper, unnoticeable if you didn't hold the note close and breathe deeply.

After a moment I shook my head and dropped the note of fluid azure pen-strokes and scented jasmine ivory to the blotter on my desk. I stared at it for a moment, then, with a tight smile that told my empty office that I was in control of me, I took the nickel-plated cigarette lighter from my desk, flicked it to life and held the hungry flame to the edge of the note paper.

I was under no delusion that my office was safe from prying eyes and lock picks. Jeffrey Brighton knew who I was and I wasn't going to leave him any clues as to where I was going.

When the blackened corner had curled and the flame raced upward to the tip that I held pinched between index finger and thumb I turned the sheet to make sure that all of the writing had been consumed. Satisfied, I dropped the ash and single remaining scrap of paper into the trash can beside my desk, watching to make sure that it went out.

For all of the emotion that she had brought up in me, the message itself had been simple: she wanted to meet me at the *Bourbon and Branch* at one-thirty. I didn't like the idea of going back to the same place but there wasn't enough of a reason to argue against it. Maybe it was on her way to her next stop. Maybe it was close to where she was going to be earlier in the night. Maybe she thought the lighting made her look better. I doubted the last: I was willing to bet that she knew how to look like a million bucks anywhere.

The fact that I wouldn't be able to get a message to her now to change the meeting place clinched it. I was going to be making another trip to the place that had been a safe speak-easy throughout the Prohibition years.

Before I made my way back to the tables in the red-flocked dining room of the *Bourbon and Branch* I took a detour to the waterfront. Stan was perched like a bird of prey on a stack of crates behind his steam table. The racing form in his hand was stained and I could see circles and strike-outs on the side that faced me. He tapped a pen against his temple as he studied the page before him like a fiancée considering a collection of engagement rings.

"You're never going to hit the long shot so you might as well give it up," I said.

"Look who's talking," he snorted. "You been lookin' for the big pay-off long as I knowed you." He didn't stir from his seat.

"And see how well I've done?" I made my way behind the steam table and reached below the counter for a cardboard cup. I filled it with chili from the steamer and popped a lid on it. I stuck a plastic spoon in my coat pocket and fished out a five. Taking the cigar box from the shelf beside Stan I flipped it open and dropped the bill inside. The .38 was conspicuous in its absence.

"Where's the roscoe?"

Stan shifted his skinny carcass on his perch. "Got stole." He seemed to hesitate as though he were going to look at me, then he shook his head and circled something vigorously on the form. "I gits another one tomorrow."

He was lying. No one was going to walk away after stealing from Stan. Times were hard and he had hocked his protection. Stan was known to be a shooter. The odds on someone trying him were slim. The odds on someone trying him without a gun were zero. I pulled the chrome-plated .45 automatic from my pocket and put it on top of the five.

"Two bucks," he said without looking up from his form.

"Yeah," I said. "It's been two bucks forever." I closed the box without taking anything out.

"Grab some napkins," he went on.

"You telling me that you're getting generous?" I asked. I grabbed some of the thin, wheat-colored paper napkins and stuffed them on top of the spoon in my coat. Picking up the cardboard container of chili I stepped around the end of the counter and started off into the darkness.

"I'm telling you that you is a slob," Stan said.

"Hope your horse breaks a leg," I said as the fog enveloped me.

"See you tomorrow."

Notebook 24, Entry 22

I made calls to some of the other hires in town and conveyed the badge's condolences and concerns then cooled my heels at the *Bourbon and Branch* until the waiters started putting chairs on empty tables. They were giving me and the other die-hards quiet, pointed looks so I paid my tab and headed for the door.

Being stood up by a client wasn't something that I had never been through before but this time I had let myself look forward to smelling the faint jasmine of her perfume and to hearing the mix of accents that labeled her speech like stickers on a steamer trunk. When she didn't appear I felt like a kid who got to the theater too late to see the feature and was left with the memories of the previews from last week. I stepped out onto the sidewalk, set my cup of Stan's chili on the parking valet's table long enough to tie the belt of my trench coat around me and stand my collar up against the damp.

"Cab, mister?"

I looked back at the source of the question. He was twenty. Maybe. Thin and seemed thinner in the black vest and dimmed lights. His pale face seemed to float in the air.

I shook my head. "I'm going to do some walking," I said.

It was a San Francisco night like any other, but maybe a little more so. The fog seemed to be heavier and it swallowed sound and light more quickly – a hungry grey ghost that haunted the city and wouldn't let it ever forget the things that had gone on in the death shroud that never left its shoulders. I made my way to the corner of Jones and O'Farrell and looked back at the now-closed *Bourbon and Branch*. The lights were out and it was as if the place didn't even exist anymore. I made my way down to the corner of Bush and Van Ness, between Japantown and Lower Nob Hill.

There was no particular reason to go there at two in the morning. No bars. No one to talk to. Just a used car dealership, a coffee shop, and a deli that would be serving breakfast in a few hours. I had found myself walking those blocks a lot over the last few years. It was quiet and no one there knew me. I could walk and think and not worry that someone was going to try to even a score with me while I wasn't paying attention.

I wasn't sure what to make of Elaine Merriman or of Jeffrey Brighton. Nothing seemed to add up in this screwy case. If Brighton didn't have the letter why did she insist that he did? If he did, why was he willing to pay me to get it from someone else? I was busily not paying attention when I turned up an alley and realized a moment later that I was going to have to turn around or learn how to climb a concrete wall without a ladder.

Notebook 24, Entry 23

I turned back just in time to see them step out of the fog and shadows.

Sure, it takes the equivalent of an idiot rookie on the stupid side of slow and probably half-drunk thrown in to let himself get cornered in a dead-end street with nothing but a ten-foot concrete block wall boxing him in at one end and a trio of more-than-capable broken-nose types at the other. Being un-armed put the cherry on.

Okay, so that's what it takes. But I don't like calling myself things like that. I wouldn't be surprised if Lt. Martinelli called me that and maybe worse the next time that he saw me. I told myself that I wouldn't care so much then. Dead men don't care about things like that. As far as I could tell, dead men don't care too much about most things.

I thought about what it was that I still cared about – just what was the tote on the score card that kept me from being in the 'might as well be dead anyway' column of the big book. Not much. A cheap apartment that I was never in. An office that I was rarely in. A trench coat that I could call home. The rest, well…

So maybe this was it – the night that I let myself in for the last slumber. Maybe I had planned it or let it happen without wanting to admit it. The head-shrinkers could have a field day with it. 'Private-Eye Probably Promoted Own Passing'. Suicide by hood.

But then – okay – I like Stan's chili. I curled my lips back over my teeth and popped the top off the cardboard container I had picked up at the stand of the closest thing to a friend I had.

Stan would understand. Well, in fact, he wouldn't care. "Dinner's on you, pal," I snapped. A cloud of spicy steam jetted up just before I tossed the contents into the nearest thug's kisser. He didn't scream. He didn't run away. He was a professional. And he was, for a few seconds, blind. He didn't see the knuckle-duster come out of my pocket and jab at the lantern he called a jaw. He probably didn't even realize that his lights had been put out as he dropped like a pole-axed cow, first to his knees, then, like a slow-motion movie of a redwood coming down, face first onto the rain-slicked asphalt.

I had my mit in his pocket faster than an IRS agent at a tax-amnesty party. The snub-nosed .38 seemed to jump into my hand like an ex-lover who had come to her senses. The curved, smooth walnut grip nestled into my palm for a snuggle and the hammer offered itself up to be stroked. As I brought it up I could smell the gun-oil. Slightly sweet and slightly metallic. It was a good mix of business and pleasure perfumes that meant both serious, sweaty work and a promise that we'd still be together in the morning if I held up my end of the deal.

The sleeper's partner in the too-tight tweed had closed the distance, his gat was clear of his jacket and the barrel was coming up in a most un-friendly manner toward my favorite fedora. Before he could finish the thought I had pointed and squeezed just like my old drill instructor had taught me and the Smith and Wesson sang my favorite tune.

The gout of blood exploded back at me from where the bullet ripped into his knee. A dark red halo sprayed out for an instant and colored the dim black and white. I breathed in the plume of cordite and gunpowder and it coursed through me like the smell of beer stoking the thirst of a factory worker after a long shift.

This guy wasn't above a scream. The gun dropped from his hand and clattered to the street as his priorities were shifted by the sudden introduction of agony. By the time that he had hit the high notes he had dropped to my level where I was still crouched. I grabbed him by the lapels and twisted him until his beefy back was between me and the remaining bruiser: the one with the narrow face and darting eyes. The one with the .45 in his hand. His first shot went wild and I took a spray of crimson from the sleeper's body. At least he hadn't been awake when he had died.

His next round would have ended my night permanently if it hadn't been for my tweed covered shield. The heavy, slow slug punched into his back and he began to scream and jerk. I had my hands full just trying to keep him between me and certain death.

The .45 barked twice more and the screams went silent like a Philco when you pull the plug. The automatic's barrel spit orange-yellow tongues of fire like a Chinese dragon and I could feel the heat from the burning gases as the shooter continued to rush forward, his long, thin finger still jerking the trigger. He was close enough now that I could see the slide jack back and the spent casings leap out of the side port to clatter onto the street like a killer's castanets. The thuds that slammed into my press-ganged protector made him jolt and stiffen. The bullets sent to me had found a different home and I was no longer holding a man by the lapels – I was holding onto a corpse.

He had gone from being a useful bone-breaker for his boss Jeffrey Brighton to being a high velocity ballistics intercept specialist for me – from bad guy to bullet catcher in one not-so-easy lesson. From somebody's something to a sandbag.

The shooter didn't seem to be fazed by the turn of events, but now that it was down to just the two of us we were both settling into the dance. I could see his chin lift slightly as he focused his eyes on mine. He could see his only good target: my *cabeza*. And he was going to do it right and right now.

My right arm came up under my shield's limp left while I used my free hand to keep him steadied in front of me. The revolver in my grip just cleared the tweed-covered armpit. My thumb dragged the hammer back to its locked stop.

The .38 sounded like a pop gun after the thunder of the .45 but it still only took one shot to end the debate about who was going to make it home and who was going to take a ride to a meat locker. I gave him an extra argument anyway.

      The first bullet took him in the center of his chest and he staggered. The second one punched through the left side of his face; the lead drilled through from just below the sharp cheekbone and blew through the rear of the top of his head taking hopes and dreams and brain and bone with it. He crumpled like a dropped accordion and even let out one last, long sigh. His coda was a broken note.

Notebook 24, Entry 24

It was noon before the cops cut me loose and I made my way back to my place. I left my clothes where they fell and was down to my skin by the time that I made it to the bathroom and turned on the shower. I let the spray pound me until I felt the muscles unwind.

I wanted to just close my eyes and forget but I had learned better a long time ago. The dead linger there for quite a while.

I pulled on the heavy burgundy robe that an ex had given me and went to the kitchen. I took a paper bag out from between the stove and the cupboard, popped it open and went back to the living room.

I made quick work of emptying the pockets of the clothes I had been wearing out onto the coffee table and shoved the whole kit, shoes included, into the bag. I could still smell the gunpowder. And the blood. I folded the top down, carried the bag to the trash chute in the hallway and tossed it in. Back in my rooms I washed my hands again then poured myself a stiff drink.

Notebook 24, Entry 25

I could hear the penguins ice skating out in the living room before I was fully awake. Or maybe it was mice, all decked out in patent leathers and black tie at a dance. No, not that, either. My right hand moved out toward the bedside table, knocked over the water glass which fell onto the thickly carpeted floor as I continued to grope for the butt of my automatic.

I could hear Stan laughing. 'Where's the roscoe?' he mocked.

I forced my eyes open and drew a deep breath. The elephants in the living room were rearranging the furniture and I didn't like the way that they were doing it.

I sat up, checked the light in the room – nothing but a little bit of street light seeping in – and swung my legs out from beneath the covers. I came fully awake when my feet hit the puddle of water on the carpet.

I reached down and pulled the sheathed KA-BAR combat knife from under the bed. I unsnapped the strap and cleared the blade, moved to the door and listened. No penguins. No mice. No elephants. But there was someone out there, going through things and they didn't want to be noticed. I checked the bottom of the door. No light shown through.

They were using a flashlight, then. Good. I knew the lay-out better than they would. It also meant that, if I was fast enough, I wouldn't be facing a weapon. Since my un-invited guest had to have one hand for the flashlight and one hand to search with I would have a big advantage. I gripped the handle of the door and eased it open.

The flash of the light swung up – I threw the knife sheath at the place I guessed would be the head and charged. I held my left forearm up like I was a Roman centurion with a shield and connected with a body. I drove forward, pushing the burglar backward toward the front door. When we slammed to a stop I kept the pressure of my left forearm up, pinning the intruder, and brought the tip of the combat knife up to a throat – the back of my hand came to rest against – the curve – of a breast.

I kept the knife in place, dropped my left arm and found the light switch. The overhead bulbs glared and Elaine Merriman's frightened eyes stared back at me. I could feel her breast heave against the back of my hand as I continued to rest the knife tip just below her delicate chin.

Then I took a step back and looked down at the knife in my hand. The hand was trembling and for some reason or reasons that I didn't understand then and still don't I found myself laughing at the sight. I even looked back at Elaine and nodded from her to the spectacle so that she could get a laugh, too. But she wasn't laughing. She was still panting. She was still pressing her back against the door. A single pin-head of crimson, like a rose blooming in the snow, had welled up where the tip of the knife had rested against the alabaster of her throat.

Seeing that cut off my laughter. I stumbled back from her and managed to make my way to the chair by the wall cabinet.

I dropped down onto the cushions and let my hand that still held the knife drape over the arm rest. A second later my grip relaxed and the knife fell, blade first, down to stick in the floor. I lowered my head and rested it in the palm of my left hand.

I could hear Elaine's breathing begin to quiet and she was moving away from the door, toward me. She knelt in front of me, curled her legs underneath herself and rested her head on my thighs.

"They – they told me you were, they said that you had been – " she choked back tears.

"No," I managed, "I'm not. I wasn't. A lot of other guys were, but not me."

"I'm so grateful," she gasped. "I don't know what I would have done if you had been – "

"Killed? Murdered? Whacked? Taken for a ride?"

"Yes!" she sobbed.

I pushed her back and stood up.

"It's time to drop the 'damsel in distress' act, Love. It doesn't suit you."

"I don't understand, Jud, what do you mean?"

"I mean that I don't believe you. And I don't think that Danny Granger believed you, either."

Her sobs stopped at the mention of Granger's name. She stood and straightened her clothes. "Granger?" she asked. Her eyes showed question marks but the rest of her confessed that she was lying.

"Yeah," I said, warming up to the subject. "Danny Granger. The first guy that you were told about by those people whose opinion you value so much. If they sent you to me it would have been after you had already seen him."

"I stepped over to the cabinet where I keep the hooch and poured one, downed it and poured a second just in case the first needed reinforcements.

She bit her lower lip and was working her story up when I decided that one slug wasn't going to settle the issue for me. I tossed off the second and pushed the glass away.

"You've got to trust me, Jud," she said. Her voice was desperate but I wasn't listening to her words so much as I was watching her eyes and her hands; both were as busy as a chippie's on the night that the fleet comes in. Her hands twisted and untwisted the belt of the trench coat that she wore and her eyes skitted around the room.

"Trust you? When did trust come into this relationship? You've done nothing but hand me lies and promises and promises that we both knew were lies. You should have told me that you hired him," I said. "That would have been the smart play."

She nodded and bit her lower lip. I might have

spanked her and sent her home if she'd been anyone else. If the case had been any other case. If he had been any one else on a long list of others. Well, she wasn't. It wasn't. He wasn't.

"You knew that Brighton was in town looking for you. So you hired a P.I. to hold the letter and went into hiding."

She nodded, her eyes flitting up to check my reaction, then they went back to their dance.

"Yes, but when I got a buyer for the letter I went to get it back." She leaned toward me and lowered her eyes, her left hand extended to lay her palm against my chest. She tried to move closer but stopped when she felt me stiffen my back and move away a fraction of an inch.

"I had to do it, Jud," she whispered with a slight crack in her voice. Gone were the sultry tones of seduction. She was playing for sympathy and the orchestra was just tuning up.

"He – he – " She shook her head as though shedding a bad memory. Then she looked up at me again. "He tried to – you know?"

I could feel the ice water hit the top of my head and run down my spine. I had been hoping against hope that she would have something – anything – that I could tell myself might be believable. Maybe even true. But this story didn't have a chance. I looked away from her.

"Jud, you understand, don't you?"

I nodded. "I understand," I said. "You killed

him. But not because he tried to rape you."

"He did!" She insisted. "It was terrible! I was so scared and I just – I just – I didn't even think!"

"Oh, you thought, all right," I answered. "And you thought wrong. You got it into your pretty little head that Danny was selling you out and had set you up. Or maybe you just didn't want to pay him what you owed him. That would be an easy choice for you to make. So you killed him. But you couldn't find the letter. Then you figured that you could get me to get your letter back. Now you think that I'll believe anything that you say. Because you know that I want to."

She looked up at me and a ghost of a smile kissed her lips.

"Yeah, I'd love to believe you," I said. I let my eyes and voice go dull. "But I don't."

Her look asked where and how she had messed up.

"Danny Granger had a lover," I said. "And if you had done your homework you would have known that your story wouldn't fly."

"It wouldn't be the first time that a man – "

My open hand snapped up and froze in mid-air. Her eyes were wide and her open mouth stopped working.

"Yeah, men get tempted," I snarled. "But you couldn't tempt Granger. See, Danny's lover is an entertainer named Dixie LaBlanc. But before taking to the stage Dixie LaBlanc was known as David Patterson. The only interest that Danny had in you was that stash of century notes. And in getting the job done – because that's the kind of op he was."

She turned ashen and edged away toward the settee.

"I thought that he was going to sell me out," she said softly. "I thought that he had made his own deal with Jeffrey." She eased herself down onto the seat and for an instant it seemed that she might just keep going – dissolve into the cushions and then down through the floor itself.

"So you went to his place," I began again.

She nodded. "I told him that I wanted the letter back but he said that it wasn't there. I – "

"You tried to scare him."

She nodded.

"And you scared him to death."

"He told me that he didn't like having guns pointed at him. He just kept walking toward me…"

I waived a hand to cut her off. I didn't need to hear the rest of that.

"And last night you saw that box of Granger's things in my room. You'd seen the photo of all of us at his place so you knew whose it was. You saw the pawn ticket and you figured out where the letter was stashed. You figured that you could make a deal with Brighton. So you told him that if I was out of the picture you would produce the letter and the two of you could divvy up the proceeds. You're the reason that I have three more dead men to answer for."

"I didn't tell him to have you killed," she said softly. "I didn't want that."

I shrugged. "Maybe you did, and maybe you didn't. The difference doesn't amount to much."

I slumped back against the wall and sighed. She lowered her chin and stared at her shoes. For a long time we avoided looking at one another.

I wondered how long it would take before she decided to play the next card: pulling a small caliber automatic out of her coat pocket and settling for the letter – or the pawn ticket – before calling us quits.

I decided to spare us both before it got any uglier. "The ticket isn't here," I said. "Neither is the letter. And they won't be."

Then I pushed off from the wall and made my way across the room to stand beside her. I put a hand on her hair. "If I thought about this long enough and hard enough I could maybe come up with a story that would get you out of this mess." I took her shoulders in both hands and squeezed just a little.

"But not without putting my neck in a noose and your hand on the trapdoor lever." I searched her face for some sign of understanding but all that was written there was her plea for pity. Well, in my years I had learned that when it is time for pity it is too late. I knew that she would never be able to step outside of her own desires long enough to see it any other way. And I knew that, in time, I could get over my desire for her to do just that.

"I can give you an hour," I said as I moved away. "After that…"

Notebook 24, Entry 26

There are two kinds of sexy – there's the kind that comes from her knowing who she is and how much power she has – and that can be enough to break your stride and have you laid up until she decides otherwise. Then there is the other kind – the kind that doesn't focus on her at all – it's all about you and the way that she makes you feel, not only about her, but about you. And that kind can kill you. Because if it doesn't come through you just might not have anything left. Elaine Merriman had one of those types of sexy. Sally Hemmings had the other.

Notebook 24, Entry 27

I don't know what happened to the letter that the third president of the United States supposedly wrote to or of his illicit love. I don't care. I had collared Stu Allgood and shanghaied him into getting Danny's briefcase from the pawn and taking it to Dixie.

The note that I had sent along explained as much as I knew: there was a letter in the briefcase. It was probably worth a lot of money to presidential historians. If anybody deserved a break in this case it was Dixie LaBlanc for taking care of the man who had taken care of a lot of us.

She kept her lip buttoned about it when every shamus in 'Frisco who had ever dipped a bill with Danny Granger paid his dues at the funeral.

A week later I read that a woman named Audrey Paskill had been arrested and charged with Danny Granger's murder.

Lt. Martinelli of the Homicide Squad had issued a statement that his department had acted on an anonymous telephone tip.

Two columns over was a story about a man named Jeffrey Brighton who had been found dead in an abandoned car in the foothills. There was a torn piece of ivory colored paper still in his hand. I knew that I had come within an ace of being found in a car in the foothills.

Still, I remember the taste of Elaine Merriman's kisses and the way that she made my heart race like a kid on a bike tearing down Telegraph Hill.

Sometimes I still let her take my breath away.

The End

We hope that you have enjoyed this volume. The following is the beginning of the first Jud Carson novel-length mystery, _Dead Duck_, which contains the bonus short story, _Gas Money_.

You may also want to consider these titles:

Dead Deutsch,
A Jud Carson Mystery Novel

Sin in the Camp
(POARAR Award Winner)

Reservoir Road

The Legend of the Firedrake,
Part One: To Find a Dragon

*from **Dead Duck**:*

Chapter 1

"Sure, you can bump some schnook off. You can do it any way your imagination runs. Poison. Garrote. A bullet in the brain. A carefully placed foot while the two of you wait for the subway train.

"Killing is the easy part.

"But getting away with it can be murder. Not because you didn't use enough arsenic, or introduce enough bullets to ensure lead poisoning to the terminal state, but because you didn't leave the light switch in the right position. Or you didn't pick up the laundry on Tuesday. And you always pick up the laundry on Tuesday.

"Or, maybe you got blood on your favorite jacket and had to get rid of it. And everyone knows just how much you love that particular jacket. And they notice.

"Get the idea? It's not the big things like means, opportunity and alibi that send people away for the BIG ONE, it's the little ones, the ones that even murderers themselves don't notice.

"That's why even after years, long after everyone has given up all hope of solving the crime, those little traces remain, and a good detective, private or on the public tab, can spot these little oversights and put them together.

"I've been spotting those little mistakes long enough to pay more attention to the guy in the tux whose cufflink is missing than to the rattled little dope with the blood all over his hands.

"Vera Clausen was a rich woman, a recent widow, and an adolescent's fantasy come to life. But it was the fact that it looked like whoever had cancelled her husband's health plan was going to get away with it that convinced me to take the case."

Alley of Darkness, Ally of Death
Jud Carson, P.I.

Claire closed the book and studied the garish, 1940's pulp novel cover, letting a smile stealing onto her full lips.

She turned her head to look through the window of the Benton Drug and Sundries, and watched as Ira Anderson wrote a parking ticket on an undoubtedly out of town sedan. He hitched his worn, tan uniform trousers up on his thin hips as he put his ticket book away and made his way back to his patrol car.

Behind her, Joel Petrie, the drug store's owner and operator, swatted lazily at a fly. And, she knew, studied her long, firm legs.

She let him have a few more seconds before turning and going to the counter with the book in her hand.

"Anything else, Mrs. Hornsby?" Joel asked, looking a little sheepish, like a little boy caught with his hand in the cookie jar.

She got the latest "*Cosmo*" and waited while he rang the total up on the gold-painted cash register. At the door she paused and, with feigned clumsiness, let the bag holding her purchases slip from her hand and fall to the floor with a distinct *slap!* She hesitated, then, slowly and deliberately, bent from the waist and picked them up.

When she stood up, she pushed through the door and onto the sidewalk, smiling wickedly to herself and imagining the look on Joel's long, deeply creased face.

□□□

"No way, Claire," Dare Colfield said for the tenth time. "You've got to forget this idea altogether."

"Dare, you're my lawyer, and my friend, and I know that you have only my best interests at heart. You are probably the only friend I have in this state."

Colfield started to protest but she waved him off, gathered herself and continued.

"Since Edmund's - since he was - since this awful mess began - you have stood by me. You seem to be the only one to believe I had nothing to do with it. If it weren't for you, I would no doubt be in prison right now."

She paused to retrieve her lace handkerchief from the Gucci bag beside her.

"I know that you don't want me to go ahead with this, but I must insist. It is the only way to fully exonerate myself in the eyes of the citizens of Benton. And it is the only way to find out who really killed my husband."

Here she dabbed lightly at her clear blue eyes with the handkerchief.

"Claire," Colfield began after a moment, his voice as soft and concerned as he could make it, "you don't have to appease these people, with the money from the estate you could move away from Benton. Far away."

As far as several million dollars can take you, he thought. "If you do this, it'll just stir the whole thing up again."

"But I want to stay in Benton, Dare, and I want to know who killed my husband."

Colfield knew better than to argue that point.

"But why this guy?" He held up the book she had given him when she had arrived.

The lurid cover showed a man in a trench coat bent over an obviously dead figure, a streetlight overhead making an island in the fog. *'Alley of Darkness, Alley of Death'* was blazoned across the top.

"Dare, don't be so dismissive; the man is a licensed detective. It says so on the cover."

"Clair, there are a lot of licensed detectives. Most of them don't write pulp novels."

"His writing shows that he has imagination. I think that imagination might be very useful."

Colfield glanced at the spine of the book."But this is fiction!" he said pointing to the caveat on the crease.

"He explains that." Claire took the paperback, flipped it to the preface and handed it back to the lawyer.

" 'There are enough lies in this book for me to call it fiction. Anybody who would have a right to sue me will have a hard time trying to prove anything. Jud Carson, P.I.' "

Colfield rolled his eyes.

"Well, I think that pretty well sums it up," Claire said as she stood and busied herself tucking away the handkerchief. "I'll be expecting your call soon, Dare. Please, don't let me down on this."

Colfield waited twenty minutes after Claire Hornsby left his office before he started to move. He was glad she had not expected him to see her to the door since that would have meant he would have had to put his shoes back on.

This whole business of hiring a private detective to investigate Edmund's murder was aggravating enough, but on top of that he would now have to track this guy Carson down. And the only thing that he had to go on was a pulp detective story with a garish cover.

"Jud Carson is a licensed private investigator living and working in California," the blurb ran. With any luck he might have no luck at all in finding this Carson and Claire could forget the whole issue. And maybe she would notice him in a less professional way.

But he would have to make some gesture.

And that meant he would have to call Benny Tuptil in California. He shuddered to think about it. All the way through law school Colfield and Tuptil had shared a dorm room. Benny Tuptil with his ever helpful manner, his constant jokes and incredible belches.

Colfield could almost hate him.

"Dare?" Benny yelled. "Dare, you old son-of-a-what are you up to? Better than that, where are you? The airport?"

It took a few minutes to get across to Benny that Colfield wasn't in California, but Benton, and why he had called. Once Tuptil knew as much about Carson as he did, Colfield did his best to end the conversation, certain that with the matter securely in the hands of Benny Tuptil, it would soon become a dead issue. He could tell Claire that he had tried to find Carson and was expecting a call back any day. Tuptil would be too embarrassed to call back and tell him of his failure.

He sighed contentedly and leaned back in his chair, looking about the quietly lighted office while waiting for an opportunity to end the call to Tuptil.

Tuptil had started recounting an incident involving Colfield, a co-ed, too much beer and a trampoline, when he was interrupted by another call.

In the moment that he was on the other line, Colfield started to hang up. The receiver was nearly in the cradle when he heard Tuptil shouting at him again.

With a shrug, Colfield moved the receiver again to his shoulder, cradled it against his neck and began cleaning his nails with the letter opener from his desk, letting Tuptil ramble as he day-dreamed about Claire Hornsby's legs.

"Got that?" Tuptil asked.

"What? Sorry, Benny, someone was talking to me."

"Carson's information. Just came in on the other line. Got a pen?"

Something cold ran down Colfield's spine, something that told him that things were not going to go smoothly in Benton for a while, but he reached for the pen in spite of his apprehension.

"Yeah, Benny, go ahead."

For a long time after hanging the phone up Colfield simply stared at the address and phone number on the stark white pad in front of him. He had underlined Carson's name half a dozen times, considered crossing it out altogether, throwing it away with his newspaper, burning it out of his life with the cigarette lighter he kept on his desk.

And he thought about going to California and punching Benny Tuptil in the face.

It disturbed him that Carson might really be what the publisher claimed, what Carson himself claimed. A two-fisted type of private eye who might just take the case, who might show up in Benton and start asking a lot of questions.

And they could very well be damned embarrassing questions.

This guy could be the kind of detective that Colfield had read about when he was a kid. The kind of guy who got to the bottom of things no matter what, the kind who considered a retainer a sacred oath to find out the truth no matter who got hurt.

Colfield told himself that he was making too big a thing out of it. That kind of detective was pure Dash Hammett and Mickey Spillane.

Then he noticed the paperback still on his desk, the garish red and black dominated cover and sensational title.

His hand trembled just a touch as he opened the cover. The first line seemed to justify his fears.

"I'm not the type to distrust anybody just out of paranoia," Colfield read, "but, let's face it, in this society, a lawyer isn't just *anybody*."

□□□

About the Author:

John M. Spafford is a decorated former career Air Force intelligence analyst assigned to world-wide duties for the National Security Agency (NSA). After returning to civilian life, he took up his former occupation as a journalist and news photographer, culminating in his being named managing editor.

Mr. Spafford has earned his Paralegal certification, Bachelor of Arts degrees, *summa cum laude*, in psychology and in sociology, from the University of the State of New York, and Master of Arts from the University of Phoenix.

As a member of a forensic investigative team, Mr. Spafford brings his analytic skills to bear on criminal cases presented both pre-trial and post-conviction.

Mr. Spafford has taught at the college level and all levels of public education. He currently teaches high school subjects in a maximum security prison in Indiana.

A professional entertainer for more than twenty years, Mr. Spafford is an accomplished magician and singer-songwriter. He is a member of the National Writers Union (UAW Local 1981), the International Brotherhood of Magicians (I.B.M.) and the American Society of Composers, Authors and Publishers (ASCAP).

www.ingramcontent.com/pod-product-compliance
Lightning Source LLC
Chambersburg PA
CBHW020643130626
46552CB00003B/1381